The Craftsman's Haunted Heart

Copyright

Second Edition, February 2025

Paperback ISBN: 978-1-961966-79-6

Published by: Carxander Publishing
Wisconsin

Dedication

When the sun and moon no longer shine, your light will still guide us home.

Opening Quote

Don't wanna let you down, but I am hell-bound. Though this is all for you. Don't wanna hide the truth. No matter what we breed, we still are made of greed. This is my kingdom come

Demons by Imagine Dragons

Chapter One

Cody

I park my brand new, sleek, red Dodge Charger in my garage. As I get out, I hear the unmistakable sounds of my brother's kids playing in my backyard. My brother is two years older than me, I'm thirty-two, and he acts like he's above me and better than me in every way possible. He's been with his high school sweetheart since they were sixteen. They have two adorable kids. He thinks he's got a better job. My parents adore him and would do anything for him.

Blah, blah, blah.

One of the things that no longer surprises me is the fact that he shows up to my house and lets himself in my backyard. It's usually when he wants to gloat about something ridiculous.

What does surprise me is my ex-wife's car parked behind my brother's in my driveway.

I don't know what fresh hell I'm about to walk into, but seeing my parents walking across the street from their house towards mine isn't something I'm prepared to deal with. Something is going on, and it's sure to annoy me.

"Great," I mutter.

"Son!" my father exclaims way too excitedly.

"Hey," I say. Maybe I should go back to work. Obviously, I'm safer there.

I own my own construction company. Timber's Construction. Named after me, of course. Cody Timber. It was one of my cocky moments. I don't regret a second of it. My brother is an executive for a tech company I've never cared to learn anything about. I don't care. He constantly brags about how much he makes. The bonuses. Vacations. The mansion he just bought.

What he doesn't know is while I live far more modestly, I make a lot more than he does. I've never cared to discuss how much I rake in. All he or anyone in my family knows is that since I got divorced two years ago, my company is still doing fine and didn't take a hit. The truth is, it grew exponentially, and I don't know why. My income is not something I've shared with anyone, though. No one needs to know. I have my splurges. My ex-wife got her settlement. That part of my life is behind me. I'm happy.

Which is the single reason I'm on such edge right now. I don't know what the fuck is going on.

"Why is my house being invaded, mom?" I ask when they reach me. I'm standing in front of my garage with my arms folded over my chest while the garage door closes behind me. You know damn well I hate surprises."

"Oh, honey, we know. This isn't for you. Your brother got a new promotion. We wanted to celebrate."

"What does any of that have to do with me? And why is Mikaela's car here?"

"Enough, son. You know she's still close to the family. We knew we wouldn't get you to go to your brother's house for this celebration. Or anywhere else, for that matter."

I roll my eyes. "That's by design, dad. Look, I'm not in the mood for this. I've had a long day and will have another one tomorrow. I want a shower, then bed."

"We don't always get what we want. Stop being selfish and celebrate your brother," my mom scolds.

I sigh and drop my arms to my sides. I shake my head as I walk to my front door. "Like he'd do the same for me," I mutter.

My parents walk towards my backyard through the gated entrance. Good. I can lock everyone out of my house, and they can do whatever the fuck they want without me.

Of course my plan is foiled. The second I get my front door open, someone is jumping in my arms. I have no choice but to step back to steady myself. Legs wrap around my waist. Arms wrap around my shoulders. My arms instinctively wrap around the person so they don't fall.

"Baby!" a shrill, high-pitched voice pierces my ears. A voice I'm tired of hearing. I got a divorce. Part of the deal was I wouldn't have to hear that voice ever again.

Well, fuck be to me, I guess.

My arms drop immediately. "Get the fuck off me before I shove you on the floor without a second thought, Mikaela. What the fuck are you even doing here?"

"Oh, come on, baby. You know I'm always included in family functions."

Bile is starting to rise from my stomach. I grip her hips and forcefully remove her from me, depositing her ass right on the floor. Unfortunately, she stays on her feet instead of actually landing on her ass.

"Leave, Mikaela. I don't want you here."

"What is wrong with you? We used to be so good together."

"Yeah. And then you fucked my best friend. Where is he, by the way? Does he know you're here right now?"

"You know he's not going to show up here." She rolls her eyes.

"Good thing, too. He'd end up with my fist in his face again. Why don't you go back to him so I can get back to my life, huh?"

"Why are you such a dick?" She crosses her arms over her chest, pushing up her tits. I once loved when she did that. Now it just disgusts me.

"A question you know the answer to." I leave her staring after me as I walk up my stairs after kicking off my shoes by the door.

I quickly shower and change into shorts and a t-shirt. I have no intention of going outside to celebrate anything. My plan is to shove Mikeala out, if she's still in my house, and lock the doors.

I stop dead in my tracks and narrow my eyes. I had the doors locked. How the fuck did she get in?

"Mom and dad," I scoff under my breath. "Of course."

"Uncle Cody?" a sweet voice asks. "You coming out?"

I look down into the brown eyes of my sweet six-year-old niece, Dezi. This girl is the best thing about her father. I wouldn't be able to deny her if I tried. I don't want to go out there, but I'd do anything for her.

"I don't particularly want to," I admit. Her lip quivers. "But I will just for you, sweet girl. Don't cry." I lift her in my arms, and she hugs me happily.

"Mean Mikaela is here," Dezi whispers.

"I know, sweet girl. But I won't let her be mean to you."

Mikaela is truly a bitch, but one of the things that pisses me off so much about her is how she treats Dezi. She gets along well with my brother's older kid, Jake, he's ten. Dezi is just never someone Mikaela seemed to like.

After an hour, I'm looking at any excuse I can to escape the bullshit happening around me. Dezi hasn't left my side, and the conversation is revolving around my brother making Senior partner or exec or something or other.

I sigh and raise my voice above the din. "Look, guys. We need to wrap this up. I need to go. I promised a friend I'd help him out with some repairs around the house," I lie. "He's a vet. Got honorably discharged for medical reasons. Shrapnel in his leg. He walks with a slight limp, and some things are hard for him to do." More lies.

"You're leaving now? It's already after six. What repairs can you possibly get done tonight?" my mom asks.

"You'd be surprised." I stand, intending to leave, but Dezi grabs my hand as everyone starts talking again. I kneel in front of her, thinking she wants a hug, but she surprises me.

"You should invite him over! What if he's hungry and needs food but is too sore to cook?"

I look at her in astonishment. It always surprises me how smart and kind she is. She's very instinctive, too. This six year old is incredible on so many levels.

"I don't think that's a good idea, honey."

"I think it's a fabulous idea," my mom pipes up. I didn't even know she could hear anything being said.

"We'd love to meet him!" Mikaela says.

I'm sure you would. I want to say those words out loud with everything I am. I don't because of Dezi.

"Come on, Uncle Cody," Dezi's sweet voice says to me. It finds its way directly to my stomach and punches me.

"Okay," I tell her without thinking as I pull her into a hug.

"Yay!" She hugs me tight before kissing my cheek.

I stand as she runs off and groan as I head for my backdoor. I don't bother locking the door because I know my mom will just unlock it if someone wants to go inside. Besides, the kids might need the bathroom.

I walk through the house and make my way to my work truck instead of my car. "What are you going to do now, man?"

I back out of my garage and head towards the only place I know I can pick up a guy.

Home Depot.

Chapter Two

Tyler

"I'm not asking. I'm telling," I say into my phone as I put a drill into my basket.

"I think it needs to be cleared with Mr. Timber."

I sigh. "Who's the Foreman at the site, Ginny?" I ask the receptionist at Timber Construction. "Me. I'm the Foreman."

"I understand, but this is a hundred thousand dollar expenditure."

"And my max decision making limit is a quarter mil. Get this done. Don't bother Cody with this. He has enough on his plate." I hang up the phone with a low growl before turning down the aisle with nail guns.

I'm Tyler Fucking Ryan. Lead Foreman at Timber Construction. People better start recognizing that name because I'm tired of everyone running to the boss for every damn decision I make. I was promoted to the position I have because I'm damn good at what I do. So good that Cody didn't fire me or attempt to get me to quit after he caught me fucking his wife. Ex wife now.

What a fucking mistake that was.

One time.

One time I let my judgment slip, and I ruined my whole damn life. I lost my best friend. I almost lost my job with the best company I've ever worked for. The single reason I didn't is because Cody actually has a heart.

I obviously don't, and I've been beating myself up for it all ever since he caught us.

I got punched for what happened. I didn't even try to block it. I just took it because I deserved it. I deserved a lot more. I've spent the past two years trying my best to make it up to him. I've gotten him so many new clients through my contacts and contacts of theirs. Word spread fast about him. After his divorce was finalized, his company just took off. I've sat back this entire time just watching it happen.

He deserves the best, and it's the least I can do for fucking up the way I did.

I haven't attempted to talk to him, though. The last time we said anything to each other was six months ago when I got promoted. He handed me my new contract, told me to look it over and sign it. If I liked it, I'd be Lead Foreman. If I didn't, then let him know what I don't like, and we'd work on it.

I didn't even look it over. I signed it right in front of him, told him I trust him, and that was the end of it. He gave me my company card and told me my approval limit was a quarter mil, which means I can make on site decisions for equipment and supplies of up to two-hundred-fifty grand.

Hence the reason getting questioned on everything pisses me off so damn much. Everyone loves going to Cody to make sure I'm not approving too much. We have a budget. I've always stuck to it. If I need something extra, I never go over my limit. I need more cement for the floor of the office building we're doing because a car drove into our construction zone and ruined everything we already laid. We have to start over.

Cody had already been informed when I showed up to the site early this morning. He already knew the order was coming. I put it in the second I showed to the site. I expected a delay until I got my cement in, but not an all day one. I'm starting to think everyone is sabotaging me.

I sigh after grabbing everything else I need for a few projects I have around my house. I start heading towards the checkout when I see Cody.

"Shit," I whisper. He looks pissed. When the dude he's talking to walks away, Cody actually looks defeated as he reaches up to rub his temples.

I stay where I am and just observe him. I've never told a soul, but I've always had a thing for him. Even after our friendship ended, the feelings I have for him never went away. I'm bisexual. He knows that. I know he's a hundred percent straight, but it's never stopped the fantasies of all the unholy things I'd do to him.

I shake my head. *Get him out of your head, asshole. You never had a chance, and you definitely don't now. You fucked that up.*

Just as I'm about to sneak by him, he catches my eye. I expect a glare, but he just looks down and runs his fingers through his hair.

Something pulls me towards him. By the time I think better of it, it's too late. I'm already next to him.

"You okay?" I ask hesitantly.

"What do you care?" he grumbles.

I sigh and run my own fingers through my light brown hair. "Look. Cody, I know you're not gonna believe me, but I never meant to hurt you. I fucked up. She was coming onto me, and you know the state I was in that day. I'm not making excuses. I really, really fucked up. You can never forgive me if you want. I know I'll never get our friendship back, but I really am sorry."

It's the most I've ever been able to say to him since that day. I'm shocked at being able to get the words that I've wanted to say for two years out in the open. Even more shocked when he nods his head. I don't say anything else. Instead, I start to take my leave.

"How many times?" Cody asks me.

I stop dead in my tracks and turn to him. "What?"

For the first time, his dark, stormy, gray eyes meet mine. "How many times did you fuck her?"

I shake my head, a little confused. "Once. You walked in as we were finishing."

He chuckles. "I thought so."

"What… does… that mean?"

He gives me a half smile. "She made it seem like a lot more. I never really believed her. She's been going around saying you're together now. But she never brings you around."

"Fuck. I swear, man. I'm not with her. She tried, but one time was it. Our friendship meant everything to me. I regret to this day what I did to you."

"Why'd you do it?"

I shrug. "I wish I had an answer. I don't. It was stupid. Selfish. I wasn't in the right headspace with my dad dying so unexpectedly. She saw what she wanted. She took advantage. Manipulated me. That's the truth. Even still, I'm a grown man. I fucked up. I own that mistake just like I own the fact that our relationship was ruined because of my actions. I could've chosen to back away. I didn't. It felt nice to have someone touch me, and I was selfish and drunk. No other words."

Cody nods, his eyes flicking to my basket. "Got some shit going on?"

"Uh, yeah. You know I have the Halloween display and haunted house. Need to start putting that up. My drill and nail gun broke on the same damn day. Had to replace them."

"Need some help?"

I raise an eyebrow. "You... want to help?"

He sighs. "Look, man. It's been two years. I don't miss her. I miss the hell out of you, though. I just want to put this behind us. Start over or something. Or just forget it happened. Ignoring her existence would be fine with me."

I can't help but laugh. "She's been gone for two years, right?"

"I wish. She shows up to family shit still. She's at my house right now. My dick brother got a promotion. I told them I was leaving. Had to help a friend. Then, Dezi said I should bring the friend to my house to eat."

I laugh again. "You've never been able to say no to her."

"Still can't. I came here to find someone who can walk with a slight limp and pretend he's ex military. Hundred bucks. Free food. Free beer. No takers."

"Sounds like a good deal. Can I get in on that?" I tease.

Cody laughs the first genuine laugh I've heard from him in a long time. "You know how my family can be. You really want to subject yourself to that shit?"

I grin. "For free food and beer? I'm down. Besides, might be fun to see Mikaela's expression when she sees us together."

Cody smiles, and my insides melt. I turn a little so he can't see what he does to me and curse myself for the millionth time in our twenty year friendship. I can usually keep it under control, but the second I lost him is the very moment my want and need for him became something wild.

Fucking ridiculous.

"If you want to come over… I… uh… I'd be happy about that. You'd make it more bearable. And I miss you." Cody keeps his head down. "I miss helping with the haunted house. I used to do that every year with you."

"I miss that, too." I pause, part of me not believing this is real. "I'd be honored. If you'll have me," I say a little quieter than I intend.

He puts a hand on my back and pats it. "Really. The honor is mine. I miss having you around. I miss my friend." He lets his hand fall, and I miss the warmth immediately.

As we walk to checkout, I'm careful to check my emotions, but something tells me this is going to end badly.

Chapter Three

Cody

"Fuck!" Tyler barks from his truck. I look up and see him with his hands on top of his head looking down at his tire.

"You okay?" I call.

"Fucking tire!" He kicks it. And then again for good measure as he drops his hands. "I don't have a spare. I just used it. Nail in the tire from the construction site. Looks like I have another damn nail in my fucking spare one."

I walk towards his truck. "Uh. There's a gas station just over there." I point to the other side of the parking lot.

Tyler looks at me. "Nah. I'll just leave it. Call a tow truck later."

"You sure? We can at least get it to my house. Let it sit there." I gesture over my shoulder to my truck. "I have a tow bar on my truck."

"I thought you had your car today?"

"I took that today, yeah. I had a meeting and wanted to look the part. But I grabbed the truck to come here just in case I picked someone up with lumber or some shit." I shrug. "My garage is a two-car."

"Right. Yeah. Mr. Fancy over here," Tyler says with a grin. "I actually forgot you had a two-car garage."

I grin back as I put a hand on my stomach. It feels like it's about to take flight. *What the fuck was that?* I know exactly what it was. I just don't want to admit it.

I clear my throat. "We'll just leave it. I'll drive you home after we come back and have it towed."

Tyler bites his lip, and my stomach flips. *The fuck is happening to me? Get a damn grip, Timber. You must be fucking tired.* Not admitting the real reason is the best option. No admission means it doesn't exist.

"Yeah, that would work, I guess. If you don't mind. I have to be on site early. And speaking of that, can you please get people off my fucking back? I try to purchase shit, and people go directly to you. I asked our receptionist to get an order in for cement so I can have it tomorrow. She's insistent on asking you, so I'm not getting it tomorrow, and this project is gonna be delayed. It's a Friday tomorrow, so that's three days of work I ain't gonna be able to do. That's gonna put us behind."

"Don't worry about it," I wave my hand dismissively. "I'll call the company and get it in. We'll have it tomorrow." I pause and grin. "Maybe I'll just make you VP."

Tyler laughs a rich, deep timbered laugh that sends shivers down my spine. "I wonder what people would say then."

I put a hand on his truck to steady myself. *Fuck. Maybe I'm sick.* Yeah. Sick. That's it.

"Let 'em talk. It's my company. Hell, you should've been VP a while ago. It would've been great for us both." I rub my head and wince slightly. "And just for the record, I'm really sorry about your dad. You needed me, and I wasn't there. We've known each other since second grade. I should've been there for you. Not off dealing with business. Maybe what happened wouldn't have."

Tyler shrugs. "Maybe it was for the best. You dropped her after. She was never good for you anyway. Only caused you heartache. Maybe in hindsight, while I still fucked up royally and never should've let things go there, perhaps it was the best option to free you from under that bitch. She would've cheated with someone. I was just there at that moment."

I look down with a small smile. Confession time. "You know, thing is, I was never as pissed at you as I should've been. Probably why I never tried to get you to quit or let you go. And why I gave you a promotion."

Tyler chuckles. "Dude. I honestly didn't know what to do with myself. I wanted to talk to you, but I didn't want you to punch me again. I would've deserved it, but I wanted this back, man. I wanted us back."

I glance at him, my smile growing just a little. I don't know why those words do things to me they shouldn't. Yes, I do. These are things I've locked down for twenty years. I've done all I can to ignore them over the years. Every time they surfaced, I went and fucked my wife until he wasn't in my head anymore.

But it's happening again.

I can't allow it to. I know he's bi-sexual. I know he's been with men and women. But I'm not. I'm straight. I just happen to have feelings for him.

No. No, I don't. I'm just happy to have him back in my life.

Right?

That's a lie. The truth is, I don't know what the fuck I am. I've never been attracted to another man. Just Tyler. I couldn't imagine doing anything with another guy, let alone kissing him or holding his hand.

Just Tyler.

Fuck.

"You okay?" Tyler asks.

I glance at him. I'm so lost in thought, I didn't even realize that we got in my truck and are halfway to my house after deciding to leave his truck in the lot overnight instead. "Fuck. Sorry, man. Just a lot on my mind. I just want Mikaela and my family gone. I love my niece, though. I'd keep her. Everyone else just needs to leave me alone."

"Well, maybe me being there will help. We can lie and say we never stopped talking or some bullshit. Not like they'd ever know, and it would put Mikaela in her place."

I chuckle. "Lie, huh? Why the hell doesn't that sound like a terrible idea?"

"Because it's a damn good one. Besides, we've come up with a lot of them over the years to get out of trouble. Remember the grass fire we started?"

I laugh. "That was a serious offense. I see that now, but back then? Naw."

"They're still probably looking for the fictitious dude we made up." Tyler grins. "That scar was a nice touch. Unique."

"Ah, yes. The scar on his cheek that made him look like he'd been in a fire or something."

"Scar tissue. An epic cover to ensure they'd never find the guy."

"My personal favorite was the tattoo on his ass that said 'firestarter'. And the story about how we knew about it."

Tyler cracks up. "Dropping his pants and pissing on the flames to put them out!" He laughs harder, and I join in.

By the time we pull into my driveway and park my truck, it feels like no time has passed at all. We're still best friends with a lifetime of memories.

And hidden feelings that I don't know I'll be able to hide this time.

Chapter Four

Tyler

"You're back!" Mikaela leaps up from her chair and practically sprints towards Cody. That is, until she sees me… Her eyes widen, and she stops dead in her tracks.

I smirk, a twinge of protectiveness and jealousy coursing through my veins as I fold my arms over my chest. "Mikaela. Long time no see, *baby*." I put exaggerated emphasis on the pet name knowing exactly what it will do to her.

Cody nearly chokes next to me but catches himself and clears his throat as he grins. "Look who I ran into?"

"Uncle Tyler!" Dezi screeches from across the yard.

I kneel down and scoop her in a hug as I stand once she reaches me. "Missed you, kid. You've gotten really big. Look at you!"

Dezi giggles as she hugs me, burying her face in my neck. "You no get to go so long with no seeing me."

"Promise, kiddo. I'm sorry. I'll do better."

She places her hands on both of my cheeks and makes me look her directly in the eyes as she adorably narrows them. No wonder Cody can't say no to her. It's fucking impossible. "You promise."

It's not a question and has me nodding my head. "Anything you say, ma'am. I'll promise you the world."

She nods, satisfied. "Good. Have dinner."

"Yes ma'am." I carry her over to Cody near the grill. Mikaela stares after me, glaring. I can't help but grin wider.

"Cody, where's the friend you were bringing back, baby?" Mikaela asks, her voice dripping with sugar. For those that know her, though, the acidity behind those words is evident.

"Quit calling me 'baby'. You lost that right two years ago. Besides, you're allegedly with Tyler. Quit being disrespectful. My friend wasn't feeling too well. Forgot to call and cancel."

"I thought you didn't want anything to do with Tyler," Mikaela rumbles. Ah, yes. The acidity is much more clear now.

I swallow my laugh. "We ran into each other. Had a talk. Lucky he happened by. My truck broke down." I set Dezi down and hand her the plate Cody made up for her.

I take the empty plate Cody hands me and start dishing up my food. When I finish, I make my way to an empty chair. Cody is behind me and sits on the chair next to me. The silence as everyone watches us is deafening. I'm living for it.

Finally choosing to put everyone out of their misery, Cody's mom finally speaks up. "Tyler. It's so nice to see you. Mikaela talks about you all the time. You're getting married soon, I hear."

I nearly choke. Cody cracks up. "You want me to tell 'em? Or do you want to, Mikaela?" Cody asks.

"I'm not marrying her," I cut in. "Who told you that?"

"What are you talking about?" Mikaela shrieks. "Are you breaking up with me?"

Here we go. I grin.

"It's one thing to tell everyone we're dating when we aren't. But telling them we're getting married? Are you fucking crazy? How were you planning on getting that over on them? Becoming all distraught and heartbroken when I don't show up at the altar?"

"Mikaela, what's going on, young lady?" Cody's dad asks with narrowed eyes.

"He's lying! He's breaking up with me right now and making me out to be the crazy one!"

"You *are* the crazy one," Cody mumbles. He's smiling like an idiot. Dezi is laughing.

"Maybe it's time for you to leave," I say.

"How dare you do this to me?" The fake crocodile tears start rolling down her cheeks.

"I didn't do anything." I look at the kids. "And we're not doing this in front of the little ones. We're not a thing. We never were."

She stomps her foot. "I thought I meant something!"

I set my plate down on my chair as I stand. Mikaela shrinks back as I grab her arm and drag her to the door of the fence surrounding Cody's backyard. Mikaela screams to let her go. I don't. Cody and his brother both follow me, but I don't stop until I'm at her car.

"I don't know what the fuck you're trying to do, Mikaela, but it ends." I let go of her arm. "Get in the car. Drive away, Mikaela. You've done enough fucking damage for one lifetime."

"Why are you being so cruel?" she screams at me.

"Wait," Cody's brother, Mark says. "You said you've been engaged to him since the day the divorce was finalized."

"I was! I am!"

Mark holds up a hand. "Yet you were always all over Cody. Struck me as odd. This makes so much more sense. You've just been sitting here trying to weasel your way into our lives. For what?"

Cody laughs. "Money. Why else? I gave her a fair settlement. Bet you she ran through it. Get out, Mikaela. You're not wanted here. Your lies were exposed. Get out."

"Really. Get out. Stay away from everyone in my family," Mark growls as he stands next to me.

I glance at Mark after seeing the expression on Cody's face showing exactly how shocked I feel His brother is actually standing up for him. In all the years I've known him, practically our whole lives, I've never once seen Mark do anything like this.

When Mikaela makes no effort to move, it's Mark who opens her door and forces her into her car.

"Goodbye, Mikaela," Cody growls. "I knew one day your bullshit would catch up to you."

She screams and throws a full tantrum complete with hitting the steering wheel as Mark closes her door. I can't help but laugh. By the time she finally leaves, we're all waving and laughing.

We turn back towards the house, but I slow Cody down and allow Mark to head towards the backyard on his own.

Cody turns towards me curiously and looks up at me. The man has always taken my breath away, but never as much as tonight. He's a couple inches shorter than I am, but still stands at an impressive six feet two. His piercing gray eyes stare curiously into my jade ones.

There it is. I knew I saw it in the Home Depot parking lot.

Lust.

For me.

Pure and unadulterated.

Wasting no time, I pull him into me and press my lips to his, The kiss doesn't start slow. Not gentle. No. Nothing about the way I feel is gentle.

I slam my tongue into his mouth like I'll die if I don't taste him. And I probably will.

Like a starving man, Cody returns the kiss with just as much ferocity. His fingers dive into my short, dirty blond hair. His tongue swirls against mine. His tight, muscular body molds itself to mine. My hands grip his ass. My fingertips squeeze it, and he moans into my mouth. My dick is suddenly solid as steel, but it's not embarrassing at all because so is his.

When we finally break away, it takes everything in me not to drag him inside and fuck him with everything I am. Make up for lost time. Instead, I kiss him again just to make sure I didn't dream the first one.

Like he's answering all the prayers I didn't know I was praying, Cody pulls away and drags me into the garage. It's dark. We don't bother with lights. There's no need for them. We can feel all we need to in the dark. He pushes me against the side door that we came through and presses his lips to mine again, but the gentle pressure doesn't last long. Not when he feels how hard I am.

Like we're animals who can't control ourselves, our tongues wage a war neither is going to win against each other. Our teeth scrape, nip, and bite at each other's lips. The only control either of us have is keeping our moans low. Our hands explore each other's body. We press against each other just so we can feel the other's hard cock pressed against our own.

"Oh, fuck...," Cody moans against my mouth when I squeeze his dick.

"I know...," I say before my lips are back on his. I don't want him to think too much and pull away from me.

Fuck. I don't want to think too much and stop this. With one hand, I unbuckle my belt. I keep jerking him as he fumbles with his own pants. Seconds later, thankfully, we both have each other's dicks in our hands. Quiet groans and moans are all that can be heard as we stroke each other while we kiss each other ferociously and hungrily.

Precome beads at my tip and his. We use it to lube each other. He gets thicker in my hand as I get thicker in his. My heart is racing. I'm about to come, and it's going to be both at an in Cody's hand, just like I've wanted, dreamed, for so fucking long.

Taking a chance, I pull him closer to me and flip us so he's against the door. With my tongue down his throat once more, I take both of our cocks in my hand and stroke them both faster and faster. My mind is spinning with a million thoughts, but none of them matter. All that matters is him and the pleasure we're both about to get.

Cody grips my wrist as we both pant, getting closer and closer to the edge. I hope he's not about to make me stop. I would for him, but it would be painful as fuck. His other hand grips my jeans. They aren't all the way down. Just enough for my dick to be free. We're both starting to shake. My back and stomach tighten. I feel a shiver race down my spine. My dick jerks, and as I kiss him, we both start to come as we groan low into each other's mouth.

I keep stroking us both, come all over my hand, as I slow, helping us both to calm down.

"Fuck...," Cody moans.

"I know...," I whisper against his lips.

We're both silent for a few moments before we both pull away. Cody turns the light on, bathing us in dimness. Cody grabs a towel from his craftsman's table and cleans up as he hands me another one.

"We can't do this again," he whispers, but I'm not sure if it's to me or himself.

"Cody -"

He looks at me, pure confusion in his beautiful, silver eyes, and shakes his head. "We can't."

And with that, he hurries out of the garage after packing himself away. I do the same, but a lot slower. I lean against the door and let out a long sigh.

"Fuck...," I whisper as I shake my own head and look down. I chuckle a little because I can't believe what just happened.

I've wanted that for a long time. Longer than I dare remember.

Leave it to me to fuck things between me and Cody up irrevocably after just getting him back in my life.

Chapter Five

Cody

(Two Weeks Later)

"Then do it. What's the hold up?" I growl into my phone. "I ordered this weeks ago."

"And I told you we had it. You canceled, Mr. Timber. That's not our fault," the asshole who is the literal bane of my existence says to me.

"We're not playing this game, Mr. Fredrickson. I never canceled my order, but you can cancel my contract. I'll find another supplier."

"Now, Mr. Timber. Let's be ration-"

I slam the phone down just as Tyler walks into my office. I glare at him. "Don't fuck with me right now, man. I'm already on a damn rampage."

Tyler holds up his hands in surrender. "Not why I came here. But since I'm here, what's going on?"

I put my head in my hands, defeated. "The Rolling project. It's one fuck up after the next. I just canceled my contract with fucking Fredrickson because he canceled by damn sheetrock order."

"Are you fucking kidding?"

I shake my head. "Nope. Said I canceled it. I never did. It was late. I called. He said it would be there today. Just got a call from Larson. It never showed."

Tyler's hand is suddenly on my back. He begins rubbing it soothingly before he starts giving me a shoulder and neck massage. I'd like to say the groan that leaves my body is because of how good the massage feels.

I'd be lying.

It's Tyler. Tyler's hands on me causes things to harden that shouldn't with a man's touch. Chills shoot down my spine, but it's not cold. It's Tyler.

Fuck, there's nothing good about this. What the fuck is wrong with me?

Everything, obviously. Everything is wrong with me.

Ever since that day in the garage, I can't stop thinking about it. I can't stop thinking about him. Especially since that was only the first time it happened. There's been a few since.

None of this is a good idea, but I'm still going to dive right into the darkness anyway.

Tyler has a couple of inches in height on me, but that doesn't stop me from turning and gripping his waist. I pull him towards my desk and push until he's sitting on it as I stand. He looks up at me wide eyed with a smirk. All my self control, the little I had, is out the window. My lips hit his with a hunger I've never felt in my life.

I moan into the kiss, but the second his arms end up around me, I'm lost. He pulls me closer. My fingers grip his hair and tug before I even know what I'm doing. This brings a deep rumble from somewhere within him that has my dick solid as a steel beam. The next thing I know, I'm the one on my desk with Tyler's cock pressing into me as he grips my thighs.

"Oh fuck." My back hits my desk. Tyler leans over me and begins ravishing my mouth all over again.

Only this time, his hand finds my swollen length. "This for me?" he growls into my mouth. His already dark eyes look almost black.

He knows the answer to that.

I arch into his hand as he squeezes my dick. "Fuck. Fuck yes!" I keep arching into his hand. It's not the way I wanted this to go, but I'll take it as long as he eases the ache.

My hips seem to have a mind of their own. With every thrust against his solid body, he rewards me with a squeeze, rub, and thrust of his own.

"That's it, baby. Fuck my hand." He thrusts his cock into mine again as he strokes me over my pants.

I nip his bottom lip and unbutton my jeans. I quickly unzip them and push them down. "Too many clothes. I'm gonna fucking come."

This earns me a low chuckle that seems to send jolts down my spine straight to my dick as he grips it and strokes it up and down in a steady rhythm. He knows what I need. He knows how to give me the release I'm craving. He's done it again and again. I push him away afterwards, and he still comes back fighting for me, for us, even though I'm being an asshole about this.

Before I can stop it, I'm shooting out streams of come onto his hand. He uses it to coat my cock. Something about the feeling of him using my come to make me slicker for him and easier to stroke makes me come a second time.

"Fuck yes, Tyler," I whisper, mindful no one in the office can hear me.

As soon as it's over, and I'm coming down from the euphoria, regret instantly sets in. Just like it always does when I end up in situations like this with him. I try to fight it off, but it's not the logical part of me that's in control. It never is.

The problem lies right there.

I shouldn't like this. I'm not gay. I like women, right? I shouldn't crave Tyler. It's so wrong, isn't it? I shouldn't want him so much.

I shouldn't be falling in love…

Chapter Six

Tyler

I sigh. "No. We're not fucking doing this, Cody." I pull him into my lap.

Ever since our hot little make out session on his desk earlier, he's retreated. Just like he always does. This time, I'm not fucking letting it happen. He's not pulling away from me again. I'm done with the game. I need him. He needs me.

Cody pushes against my chest and tries to stand, but I'm not letting it happen. I tighten my hold on him and pull him even closer. "Ty, stop. You know I can't do this. It's not fair to you or me."

"That's not what you said earlier." I kiss his neck with a low chuckle. "Or last night." I kiss his shoulder. "Or the night before." I kiss his jaw, his scruff tickling my lips. Each kiss relaxes him more and more. So, I keep doing it. "Or the night before that." I smile against his skin.

"This isn't easy for me."

"I know." I hug him even tighter. "I know it's not easy. It's a huge change. Especially for someone who's only been with women. But you did admit to me that you've gotten off to thoughts of me." I kiss his neck again.

"And regretted it instantly."

"True. But it happened. More than once. We've been together. More than once." I sway a little with him because I can tell I'm calming him. I'm getting through to him. "I know it's scary, Cody. I do. And you know I'll take this at your pace. I'll ease you into it. I'll do whatever you want. One thing I won't do, though, is let you slip back into regret. You have nothing to regret." It's the same conversation I've had with him almost every night for the past two weeks. And I'll keep having it if that's what he needs from me. "You enjoy my company, right?"

"You know I do, Tyler."

"You enjoy my hand stroking you." I grin.

Cody chuckles. "Yeah. I can't deny that."

"You enjoy my mouth sucking you off."

"Fuck, Tyler. Stop. I get it."

"And you really like sucking me off and swallowing my come." I nibble his neck and lick it.

"You know I do."

"Then what is there to regret, baby?"

That's when he finally melts into me. All of the tension from the day is suddenly gone.

"Nothing. There's nothing to regret. You're right."

"I'm always right."

Cody laughs before looking at me. "Be my VP."

I blink a few times and raise an eyebrow. "What?"

"Be my VP. I think with both of us running the company, we could really expand it into something really fucking phenomenal."

"It already is. What do you mean VP?"

"Fuck being VP. Be co-owner."

I look at him like he's grown two heads. "Cody, what's going on? You give me a good salary, but I still can't afford a half investment."

"So? Who said you need to? It's just paperwork and a rebrand." He shrugs, his eyes turning serious. "Timber Ryan Construction. Has a nice ring to it, huh? I've been thinking about it for a while. Even before the divorce. I -"

"Cody, wait. Stop a sec. Are you sure about this? You're giving me half of a company that you built from the ground up."

"Fuck, Tyler. You helped me build it. You've been there every step of the way. This company wouldn't exist without you. I should've done this a long time ago. It should've always been us. It was always meant to be."

I look down at Cody's lap. I feel his gorgeous eyes on me as I contemplate this life changing decision. I've done a lot for his company, but this makes me wonder if he knows so many new clients came to him after he divorced because of me. I question if he figured that out somehow, even though I begged people to not say a word.

I loosen my grip around him but don't let him go. "I don't know." I look up at him again. "Are you absolutely sure about this?"

"We've been discussing owning our own company since we were kids, Ty." Cody looks down at his hands and shrugs. "We should've done this together. It should've always been you and me doing this. It's one of my biggest regrets."

I cup his cheek and turn his face towards me. I softly press my lips to his before pulling away with a smile. "I'd be honored, Cody. I am honored. I've always wanted to."

He grins. "Yeah?"

I match his megawatt smile. "Fuck yes."

Cody throws his arms around me. We stay wrapped in each other's arms for a much longer period of time than I expect, but I refuse to move. I feel like Cody and I have had a major breakthrough.

"How's your haunted house coming?" Cody asks after a few minutes.

I sigh and then groan. "I keep forgetting how hard it is to put up. I get so excited every damn year, but fuck it's hard. Worth it, but difficult. Time consuming."

"Maybe we could do it together. Like we used to."

I shiver at his deep voice rumbling against my neck. "Hell, yeah. I'd love that."

"Then, let's head over there. We still have a couple hours of daylight."

I grin and get up after he jumps from my lap. "I've missed this," I say honestly. "Just hanging out with you."

"The other stuff's a nice bonus, huh?" he asks with a smirk as we walk out of my house towards his truck.

I laugh. "Fuck. The best kind. Better than money, cars, trips..." I grin.

We climb into his truck and talk about the details we'll need to iron out with me being co-owner of Timber Construction. It won't take too much to change our name to Timber Ryan Construction. Something going for us is that we have all the time in the world.

Once we reach my house, we immediately get to work. It feels incredible to use my hands building something. Bringing it to life. One of my favorite things to do is build this haunted house, but I wasn't kidding around when I said that I missed this. I love doing things with him.

"Man, I love this so much. It's like it's just back to the basics," I say as I finish hammering a nail.

"The smell of sawdust. The smoothness of the wood." Cody runs his fingertips down a two-by-four. I watch him unsure how that simple action is so arousing.

I clear my throat and turn away. I can't help but think how good those fingertips would feel stroking my cock right now. I hyperfocus on the frame I'm working on, but I can feel his eyes on me.

Each time I look up, he's looking at me, but I'm okay with that because he's hot and makes me feel like I'm a god.

Fuck, I'm already a goner for him.

Chapter Seven

Cody

I can't seem to tear my eyes away from Tyler working. I almost forgot how fun it is to work side by side with him. The way his muscles ripple under his shirt. How hot he looks when he's got little beads of sweat forming on his forehead.

He's fucking gorgeous. How has it been possible to resist him for so many years? I shouldn't have. Fuck, I've wasted so much time acting like a jackass and denying myself. By doing that, I was obviously denying him.

Not that I didn't enjoy being with women. I do enjoy it. I'm not gay. At least not fully. I inhale deeply to steady myself because that's the first time I've really admitted to myself that I have gay tendencies but like women as well.

I'm bi. I'm bisexual. Just like Ty.

I shake my head and get back to sawing the last board that needs to be cut. Once I have it done, I stack it in the pile of cut boards and start cleaning up. Once I'm finished putting everything away, I move to Tyler's side to help him finish the frame he's working on.

"Just in time. Ready to help me get this up?" Tyler asks me.

"Yeah, of course."

Once we have the frame standing and secured, we quickly get to work on the other sides of the frame and secure them. When we're done, we're well past sunset and working with only Tyler's porch and garage lights and a couple of lamps.

"We got everything secured? I ask, looking up at our work.

"Looks like it. I staked the support beams down just in case we get a storm. Hopefully it doesn't blow down. Oklahoma can get a little windy."

I can't help but laugh. "A little?" I grin at him.

He puts his finger and thumb up and squints through the very tiny slit he makes with them. "Only a little."

We both laugh and start covering the structure. We tie tarps down and stake them to the ground, just finishing when it starts sprinkling.

"True test right here. It's supposed to be a rough night," I comment.

"Yeah, maybe you shouldn't leave. Not supposed to get tornadoes, but it's gonna be nasty storms."

I smirk as we start walking to his house. "Can't stand to be away from me, huh?"

Tyler pulls me into the house and closes the door, slamming me against it. "You're fun to be around."

I don't have a second to respond before Tyler's lips are on mine. "Oh fuck," I rumble into his mouth. I've been straining against my jeans for what feels like hours. By the feel of him, so has he.

"If I take my dick out, it's not going in your hand or mouth. I'm trying to restrain myself."

"Don't." I don't know what comes over me, but I reach down and unbutton his jeans.

"You don't know what you're doing, Cody." Tyler kisses me more passionately.

I nip his lip and unzip his fly. "Fuck if I don't."

"My dick is going to be stretching your ass while my hand fucks your cock. You ready for that?" Tyler covers my mouth and steals my breath as I take his length in my hand and start pumping it. He groans as I pull my mouth away.

"More ready than you know." And I'm not lying. I want him. I feel like I've broken through a wall, and now, all I want is to feel everything I've been missing.

"Fuck, baby."

It takes Tyler less than a minute to lead me to his bedroom and have us both naked on his bed. Clothes are strewn everywhere as he positions me on my stomach with my ass in the air for him. It's my first time like this. I should feel embarrassed or something, shouldn't I?

Why don't I? Why do I want to be in this position with him?

"Are you really sure about this, Cody?" Tyler's voice exudes all of the concern I know he's feeling.

"I've never been more sure about anything," I answer truthfully. "I don't know what's gotten into me, but I want you, Tyler. All of you." I look over my shoulder at him, meeting his eyes. "I mean it."

His smile could light up a room. It's infectious and makes my lips turn up to match his own grin. He leans down and kisses my shoulder as his hand snakes its way down my back to my ass.

He straddles my legs as he sits up and drips lube on my hole. I gasp and jerk, making him groan. I'm harder than the hardest stone. He slowly rubs the lube over my pucker. The sensation of someone touching me there is almost overwhelming.

"I'm gonna go slow, baby. Have you practiced before? Buttplugs? Dildos? Pegging?"

I swallow hard as I shake my head. "Is that something I should've done?"

A low chuckle leaves his throat. "No, Cody. I just need to know how much prep you need." He slides the tip of his finger into me, and all I can do is grip the sheets as I grimace.

"Oh my fuck, Ty," I whisper as my eyes flutter closed. I arch into him when he starts slowly moving it. "Fuck." Why do I like this? Why the fuck does it feel so damn good?

"So tight," Tyler whispers, his voice reverberating into my soul. "Your virgin ass is all mine."

"You can have it." I'm losing my mind. It's clouded with lust. All I can think about is his dick slamming into me.

Why? Why now?

I've resisted for so long. Why do I want him to fuck me like neither of us have ever been with another soul before? Is this what I get for hiding myself for as long as I have? This insatiable need to be used like a ragdoll over and over and over again?

"You're ready for me."

I look over my shoulder at him. He's using more lube and slathering it on his dick. I want to ask what's taking so long, but I know he's doing it so he can push himself in easier. Tyler has always cared so much about others. It's touching that he doesn't want to hurt me, but I want him.

Need him.

I'm just about to say something when I feel the tip of his dick against my hole right before he pushes himself inside.

"Oh fuck," we both moan in unison. I close my eyes and practically fall against the bed. My body tenses at the foreign sensation, but every single part of me tingles with anticipation.

Tyler pumps his hard length in and out of me, stretching me. Slowly. He's fucking thick. It's one thing to have his thick, silk encased manhood in my mouth. It's quite another to feel it in my ass, my tightest hole.

And it's just the tip.

"Fuck," Tyler rumbles as he thrusts deeper, though still slowly and gently as he can.

All I can do is moan.

And arch.

I feel his dick twitching inside me. I know he's holding back because he doesn't want to hurt me. I'm grateful because feeling him stretch me is a little painful. It's also the greatest pleasure I've ever felt.

I reach down and try to catch the precome dripping from my cock, but Tyler stops me.

"That's my job, baby. Don't touch what's mine." He wraps his hand around my dick just as he fully seats himself inside me.

"Damn. Oh goddamn." I'm panting and gripping the sheets as I clench around the only man I've ever wanted to lose my ass virginity to.

"Just relax, Cody," Tyler says soothingly. He rubs my ass and up and down my back. His hands are on my hips. Everywhere. I feel him everywhere. "Breathe, baby."

I love his rumbly voice.

I relax more and more. I feel myself loosening my vice grip around his dick. I'm sure he can feel it, too, because he starts thrusting slowly.

The only sounds I hear are our breathing; our skin meeting; the sounds of our lovemaking. And that's exactly what it is. There's nothing rushed. Everything is a meld of perfect rhythm and pressure. It's like we're sanctimoniously performing a soliloquy that only we know.

"You feel so good," Tyler whispers. "You're gonna make me come."

Suddenly, it's like I've never wanted anything more than to feel him filling me with all of him.

"I need to feel you, Tyler. All of you."

Tyler groans. "Oh, you'll feel me. All of me."

I arch when he thrusts into me harder. I'd think he's losing control, but I know Tyler. Him losing complete control is so rare that I've only ever seen it once. And that was when he was drunk and getting his dick wet in my ex.

Tyler hasn't stopped stroking my cock since the second he gripped it, and I'm getting dangerously close to losing it all over his sheets.

"Fuck, Tyler. I… I'm gonna… Fuck… I'm gonna come!" My entire body is trembling. I'm sweating trying to hold back. My dick is so hard that I'm starting to fear it might burst. A jolt shoots down my spine. "Ah!" I shout.

"Come, baby. Come for me, Cody," Tyler commands. He thrusts harder; a little more frantically. He's so thick inside me, I know he's about to come, too.

His words are all I need for my release to shoot from me in streams all over his bed and hand. "Tyler!" I roar, my back arching like a damn cat.

Tyler grips my hip with his other hand as I come all over him. He buries himself in me and paints my insides with all he has to give. "Cody!" he yells, sending ecstasy shooting through my entire being.

When we both finish and he pulls out of me, he hugs me close to him, his come dripping from my ass. As we catch our breath, we hold each other.

Being in his arms like this is the most content I've ever been.

Chapter Eight

Tyler

(One Week Later)

I grin when I see Cody's truck pulling into my driveway. I stop the electric saw I'm using and watch him get out of his work truck. It should be illegal to look the way he does in black jeans and a dark t-shirt. Green, I think. Like the forest at night.

"Looking good, boss," I tease.

Cody gives me his best smirk. "I always look good."

"Can't deny that." I laugh.

Cody looks at the haunted house. "Looking good. You've made a lot of progress."

I grin wider as I look at our work. "It helped there wasn't storm damage last week, but it looks good so far. We just need to get that last wall up now that the roof is finished. I finished the measurements and just got the last board sawed to size." I wipe my hands on my jeans. "After this, it's just a matter of decorating all of the inside."

"Do we have help coming for that this year?"

"Do I ever? No. Just us."

I grin because I like it like that. Just us. Makes it more special. And allows me to stare at him without anyone questioning me about it. I love having time alone with him. That's all I care about. The kids coming through after we're done and having fun in the haunted house is just a nice plus.

"Let's get this thing up," Cody says as he puts work gloves on.

And just like that, we work side by side, like we haven't lost two years of our lives fucking around. It's as if we haven't missed a day in our relationship. Like all it's done is flourish and grow. Like the past two years haven't mattered.

I've got my best friend back, and gained even more.

The love of my life.

Once we have the last wall up, I grin. "It's fucking gorgeous."

Cody laughs. "Still needs some paint. But it looks a lot better with wood than it did with all those plastic tents. This year is gonna be fucking amazing. And we can keep this all. Store it for next year."

I grin wider. "I don't know why we didn't think of that before. I guess it seemed easier to do it how we were." I head for my garage and find a light. I plug in an extension cord and plug the light into it before walking back out to the small house.

"You know, it doesn't really look that big from out here, but when you go inside, it seems huge," Cody says, popping his head out what will be the exit door.

"We made it the same height, length, and depth of the tent house we did. But we said that about the tent house, too. It seemed a lot bigger on the inside." I duck inside and look around. "Yep. Definitely seems bigger inside."

There's already a light we ran inside, but this second one makes it brighter. There are no windows, and that's very much intentional. The ventilation comes from the roof being two-inches above the rest of the frame. It's something that won't be noticeable when we have everything decorated and lighted, but is very necessary because we'll be using smoke machines. We don't want people to suffocate. The smoke needs somewhere to go.

Plus, it'll look really cool from the outside when people see different colored smoke billowing from underneath the roof.

"Looks like we just need the one wall up?" Cody asks as he tests a load bearing post.

I nod. "Just the wall we wanted to do last as the entrance and house separator. The load bearing ones are all set."

"Good because I want to start getting displays up." Cody lays out our plans on the workbench.

We have plans to put different themes in each room. I have a storage shed filled with all of the displays we plan on using, and by the time we get everything into the house and the rooms we plan to put them in, it's late afternoon.

"Not that late yet," I say looking at my watch. "We could probably get the Mummy room set up, at least."

"That's the most difficult one because of that coffin the mummy pops out of. And we need to set up the chains for whoever plays him this year."

"I think it's going to be Emerson. He's been itching for it."

Cody grimaces before he laughs. "Maybe we should double up on the anchors. He's a big guy."

I laugh. "He is, but he'll love it. We do need to make the chains around his waist shorter, though, since his arm span is massive."

Emerson is an at least seven feet tall Black guy, so it's going to be a lot of work getting him in costume. Making him the Mummy instead of Frankenstein, like he usually is, will be a change I think is much needed, though. I like keeping things fresh.

Cody and I work steadily, grunting and groaning for the next hour, setting up the Mummy display. By the time we finally get electricity to it and get it up and running, we're both sweaty and exhausted. I lean against a wall as I catch my breath.

"Fuck me, that coffin is a bitch to move and hook up." I swipe my forearm across my forehead. "At least it's done."

"Finally. The rest should go smoothly." Cody leans over the coffin and makes sure everything is hooked up right.

And that's when I decide I can't take anymore.

I quickly undo my jeans and push them down my thighs. Before Cody has a second to react, I have him in my arms with his back against my chest. I undo his pants and push them down as I kiss his neck. He gasps when I nip it.

"Working side by side with you has driven me crazy for years," I rumble against his jugular as I walk him to the work bench. It's nice and sturdy. I built it myself. I'm not worried about it breaking when I turn Cody around and sit him on it.

Cody grins. "For the first time, I can be honest and say same for me. I can fantasize and not have to shove the thoughts deep."

"Something's about to end up deep." I pull his pants around his ankles. "Balls deep." I'm not fighting with boots. I don't care if his jeans are still partially on or not as long as I can get to his ass.

I lift his legs and put them over my shoulders. His jeans are still around his ankles, so I duck between his legs so the jeans are behind my head. I spit directly on his hole and my dick. I use one hand to lubricate myself with my spit and the other to get him ready. I don't bother coaxing his pucker open for me. I use the spit and push two fingers into him instead.

"Holy fuck!" he shouts as his head drops back. He grips the end of the table as I thrust my fingers into him. I use more spit to make him wetter and easier to enter.

When he's finally ready, I pull my fingers out and slam my throbbing cock into him, giving him very little warning. I fucking need him. I need to feel him stretching around me more than I need my heartbeat. Fuck, he is my heartbeat. Without him, I'll die.

"So damn tight…," I rumble. I put my arms around his legs. His jeans hit my shoulder blades with each thrust. Cody reaches for his dick, but I growl and swat his hand away. "Mine."

"Fuck, Tyler. Jerk it already." He's barely hanging on. It makes me grin.

"When I'm ready."

I shift my hips just enough to hit him at a different angle that I know drives him wild. I know my man, and I know him well. I still have a lot to learn about all his pleasure, but I'm a quick study. I know exactly what he needs just by being in tune to him. Memorizing him is as easy as memorizing my favorite song. He is my favorite song.

Like right now.

The precome leaking from his red and twitching cock tells me he's more than ready for me to touch him. I thrust harder, faster, and deeper, being sure to hit his spot each and every single time I slam into him. His eyes roll back in his head the second my hand wraps around his length.

"Fuck…," he moans.

"Don't you dare close those eyes. Look at me when I fuck you."

Cody grins and does as told. His eyes lock onto mine as I stroke him at the same rhythm I'm fucking his ass. He tightens around me, making me groan. I use his precome to slick his dick as I stroke it, and just that action has my mouth watering to taste him.

I give him a few more hard thrusts before I start spilling jets of my come into him.

But I don't stop stroking him, and I hold his gaze.

"Fuck!" I roar. "Cody!"

"Damn, you're hot when you come," he rumbles.

I pull out slowly and watch my come drip from his ass as I lean down. I take his dick in my mouth with a low groan. "Come for me, Mr. Sexy Company Owner, sir." I grin around his dick before immediately sucking him.

"Oh fuck, yes." He grips my hair and holds me so his cock is touching the back of my throat. He comes hard, satiating me with all of him. I swallow around him like he's my life's blood.

Once we both come down, I help him pull his jeans back up before doing the same for myself. As I watch his face flush a beautiful just fucked color, I realize that all I've ever wanted has been right in front of me. I've missed him so fucking much. Like the last two years have been nothing but gray, downcast, rainy skies.

Moving on from him would never have been possible.

Not when he's emblazoned in my mind for all of eternity.

Chapter Nine

Cody

I finish staking down the tarp we just finished putting up to protect the house from the storm we're supposed to get and look up at the sky as the wind picks up.

"It's looking pretty ugly, babe," I say to Tyler as I stand.

He looks up at the sky and comes to stand next to me. "Yeah. Definitely some angry clouds." He turns and looks behind us. "Storm wall is coming in hard. We should probably get inside." He tests the tension on our stakes and tarp.

"Goes down about -" I'm cut off by the sudden angry wail of the emergency siren, and immediately look around.

Tyler takes my hand and pulls me after him as he starts running. He has a storm shelter behind his house. "I don't see anything, but I'm not chancing it dropping on us!"

"Couldn't agree more!" I keep my eyes on the sky anyway. I don't trust the alarms. They're supposed to go off and give enough time for people to get to safety. They usually don't go off until a tornado is on the fucking ground.

Once we round the corner, the wind picks up even more as the clouds unleash a torrent of rain that slices across my skin. As Tyler and I run towards his storm cellar, it feels like the wind picks up even more.

"Oh shit!" Tyler says as he slows.

Keeping my hold on his hand, I slow with him and follow his gaze. Underneath his back porch is a small, midnight black kitten. I don't even know how he saw it while we were running, but that's something I love so much about Tyler. He's incredibly observant. He sees things that a lot of others can't.

We both look at the sky. The sirens wail. The wind kicks up dirt from all around us. The rain pelts us.

"No time! It's dropping!" Tyler yells.

"I can't leave it!" I let go of his hand. There's a funnel cloud near us that's dropping, but I won't leave the poor thing to fend for itself out here.

"Cody!" Tyler barks.

I run towards Tyler's house. The kitten is trembling. It looks scared as hell, but it's watching me. I hope it doesn't dart further under the stairs, or I'll have to leave it. "Don't make this hard, little one. We don't have time."

I'm soaked. The rain is getting harder. It's starting to feel like glass, but that might be the dirt getting kicked up by the wind. Maybe it's both.

"Cody!" Tyler yells.

I can hardly hear him. I reach the porch and kneel down for the kitten. It doesn't run. Instead, it jumps into my arms like it can sense safety. I quickly turn and take off towards Tyler and the storm shelter again as the kitten's claws dig into my chest where I have it cradled. I look up and can't see the tornado, but I know Tyler can. I know he didn't follow me so he could keep an eye on it and have my back. If things got too dangerous, not like they aren't now, he'd be able to tell me.

The second I reach him, he's taking my hand again. His eyes barely leave the sky as we both run towards the shelter. Once we reach it, he opens it and pulls me into it. I quickly move down the stairs. Tyler follows, closing the door behind him as I take out my phone. I use the light to illuminate the dark area. Tyler finds his kerosene lamp and lights it. He holds it up to the doors and nods before turning back to me.

"We're locked up tight. Safe and sound." He looks at the terrified kitten burrowed against my chest.

"I couldn't leave it, Ty."

He shakes his head. “I didn’t want you to. But baby, fuck. You could’ve gotten us all killed out there. That tornado is right on us.”

I jump a little when the door rattles, as if emphasizing his words. “I couldn’t leave it, Ty.”

His hard expression softens. He walks towards me and gives the kitten’s head a pat before he starts petting it. “I know, baby.” He scratches behind its ears. The kitten starts to loosen its grip on my shirt with its claws. “Are we adopting a boy or girl?”

I grin. “I don’t know. Let’s find out.” I carefully extract the kitten from me. It mewls in protest and tries to scurry back into my chest, but I hold it up.

Tyler looks and chuckles. “Of course it’s a girl. You always were such a ladies man.” He grins as I hug the kitten back against my chest. She seems to like my heartbeat.

I smile and nuzzle her. “What are we naming her? Because I’m not letting her go.”

Tyler chuckles again. “She has a gray streak on her bottom. Kinda reminded me of a wisp of smoke.”

“Smoky it is.”

We both look up at the shelter door as we sit down on the cot he has against a wall. He sets the lamp on the small table. The doors are still shuddering, but it’s likely the tornado has passed.

“Fuck, I hope it didn’t take the house.”

I nod. “Yeah.”

He hugs me to his side as I comfort the kitten. We fall silent as the storm rages on above us. I know he’s not talking about the haunted house we’re building. He’s talking about his actual house. His family home. He grew up in this house. My family used to live right next door, but they moved into my neighborhood a few years ago just because they wanted to be in a gated community. Tyler’s house holds a lot of memories for us both.

He’s also put in a ton of work to make it his own while still keeping the integrity of it. I’m sad I wasn’t a part of that remodel with him, but he did an incredible job. The house definitely screams that it belongs to him.

Just as I do.

I smile at that thought as I rest my head on his shoulder. “This is nice. Despite what’s going on out there.”

Tyler squeezes my arm. “It’ll suck if it took the house, but you’re all I care about. The house is just a house. My home is, always was, and always will be wherever you are.”

I smile as he leans in. His lips touch mine, a little rough, but soft and everything I’ve ever wanted a kiss to be. His hand cups my cheek, and I love the intimacy of it as much as I love it on my dick. He deepens the kiss, his tongue lashing mine.

Just as he pushes me back, Smoky mewls.

I chuckle. “Glad she reminded us she’s here.”

“Cockblocked by a cat.” Tyler grins as he looks up. “I’m sure it’s passed by now.”

“I don’t hear any wind or anything. Just a light breeze and some rain.”

“I’ll check.” Tyler stands and climbs the stairs. He cautiously pushes the doors up, but keeps the latch on. After a few moments, he unlocks it and pushes it open a little more before he finally opens it all the way. “Coast is clear.” He looks down at me and holds his hand out.

I stand and shut the lamp off. I hang it right where he had it, and take his hand, the kitten still snuggled in my chest. He guides me up the stairs and out of the storm shelter. It’s sprinkling and dark now, but the wind is barely a breeze. It smells fresh. Tyler locks the door to the shelter as I look around.

“It didn’t take your house,” I say.

Tyler turns in a slow circle. “Didn’t cause a lot of damage, did it?”

“We were lucky,” someone says from behind us. We both turn to see a couple of neighbors who have also come out to survey the damage.

“Very lucky,” another one says.

“It was a small one,” another says as he hugs his very pregnant wife to his side. “We lost part of our roof.”

“We’ll take care of it,” Tyler says before I have a chance to.

I smile because it’s exactly what I would’ve said.

As we walk with the neighbors to the front of the house to survey as much damage as we can, I know we’ll have our work cut out for us, but just like our relationship, I wouldn’t have it any other way.

Chapter Ten

Tyler

(Two Weeks Later - Halloween)

"Enjoy the haunted house…," I say ominously with a wicked grin. I'm dressed as the Grim Reaper.

Cody is on the other side of the door to the haunted house dressed as Dracula. We both pull the black curtain aside just as someone inside screams.

Cody gives his own wicked smirk. "Have fun," he rumbles.

The two kids go in with trepidation while their dad winks at us on his way in.

I've been doing this house for years, but this is the best house yet. Cody and I get friends and coworkers to dress up and play different characters inside. On the outside, there are two more people at the end handing out candy to everyone who comes out the other side, including the parents.

This is my favorite time of year.

The past two years haven't been the same without Cody. It wasn't the same. We've always done this together. Doing it without him didn't feel real. This is the first year that I've really had my spark back. It feels good.

"We really went all out this time," Cody says to me once we let the last kid in line go into the house.

"I'm glad. It needed to be bigger and better than ever this year. Now that I have you back."

Cody grins. "Not as fun without me?"

"Babe, not even a little bit. It was like I was going through the motions every damn day."

"Same."

We both grin when another kid screams. We look towards the haunted house as I laugh. "This has been the best year so far."

I smile. "Not just because of the haunted house, I hope."

"No way. It's because of you." I take his hand in mine and pull him close. His arms wrap around me so naturally. When our lips meet in a sweet kiss, I have to force myself to pull back before I maul him in front of everyone.

"All clear!" one of my buddies yells from inside. It's followed by a chorus of hollers and cheers. That means there's no more people in the house. We're good to breakdown.

We put in a lot of work for one night, but we all love it. Seeing the joy on the kids' faces is the best thing about this holiday.

Well, one of them, at least.

We all work together to break down the easy stuff. Once we have all of the lights down and fog machines put away, it's nearly midnight.

"Damn, man," Brody, one of the guys we work with, says. "Didn't realize I could be so tired at midnight."

"You all did fantastic. I think it was a huge success," I say. We all take a drink of our celebratory beer.

"We're saving the frame for next year, so no knocking it down this year?" Cody says. "We can can take care of that ourselves, though." His eyes meet mine, and I grin.

He wants more time with me.

"Next year, we should hire a makeup artist," another buddy says. "Not just masks. Really get into it. Maybe we could make this a bigger annual event. Do it all month."

"Now we're talking," I say as I finish off my beer.

"Alright. Thanks, guys. Everybody, go home."

Cody takes my hand and drags me into the house as we all laugh. I know what he wants, and they very obviously do as well. The second the door is closed, he has his lips against mine. His hands devour me as they find their way to my dick, as mine does to his. Clothes are quickly shedded as we stroke each other.

It's only been a few weeks, but already we've taken massive steps in our relationship. It's like we've waited for so long for each other that we don't want to wait anymore. We've waited too long as it is. Lost too much time.

I'm co-owner of *our* company. It's been a long time coming. We're in the process of changing our name to Timber Ryan Construction. Everyone is treating me with a lot more damn respect.

Cody isn't hiding our relationship to anyone. It's like when he finally admitted to himself that he wants me, he wasn't holding that back to anyone. He's told his family, everyone we work with, friends, and even strangers just by holding my hand wherever we go.

"I'm fucking in love with you, Cody," I growl against his neck while I thrust my dick against his and stroke them both.

"I love you." His nails scrape across my shoulders as he thrusts his cock against mine.

"Marry me."

"Abso-fucking-lutely." Cody takes my hand and tugs me to the bedroom.

Our bedroom.

He moved in right after the tornado hit. It didn't take my house or the haunted house, but it did take his. It caused a lot of destruction in his neighborhood. His parents lost their home as well, but they moved in with Cody's brother. Everyone seemed happy about it, and our company got a lot of the contracts to rebuild the damaged homes.

"Not even gonna think about that?" I ask, slightly more than a little surprised that he agreed to marriage so quickly.

"Nothing to think about. I want you." He pulls me on top of him when we reach the bed, and before long, we're a tangle of sweaty limbs and hot breath as I pound into his tight ass.

After our simultaneous release, I pull him against me. We're silent for several moments before I finally break it. "You're serious? You'll marry me?"

"I'll marry you right now, if that's what you want, Tyler."

"After just a few weeks?"

"We've known each other our whole lives. And I'm pretty sure I've loved you almost that long. This is right. I feel it. I know it better than I've ever known anything. We're it."

I crash my lips to his again and again in a melody of ferocious devotion. It doesn't take long before I'm fucking him once more. It's like we're absolutely unable to get enough of each other.

I wouldn't want it any other way.

Finally… finally, everything I've wanted my entire life is in my arms.

The End

Help turn this book into an audiobook narrated by the fabulous Nowhere Eternity!

www.nowhereeternity.com

Kickstarter runs through May 2, 2025!

https://www.kickstarter.com/projects/melonyannauthor/the-craftsmans-haunted-heart-audio-by-nowhere-eternity

Other Books By Melony Ann

The Beautiful Dream Series

Available Now

Loving You
My Love, My Heart
Softening Lyric
Undercover Temptations
Captain Charming
Breaking Boundaries
Crashing Into You
Tactical Inferno
Ravishing Our Queen
Cherished By The Texan
Unveiling Our Passions

Box Sets Available

The Beautiful Dream Series: Box Set: Part 1
The Beautiful Dream Series: Box Set: Part 2

The Crane Family Series

Available Now

The Reluctant Mafia King
Sweet Lies
Billion Dollar Love Story
Be Mine
Protecting Her
Dangerously Forbidden Love
His Heart
Love In The Dark

Box Sets Available

The Crane Family Series

The Deimos Trilogy

Available Now

Connor's Legacy
Aryan's Alpha
Kade's Redemption

Box Sets Available

The Deimos Trilogy

The Forbidden Temptation Series

Available Now

The Detective's Forbidden Temptation
The Running Back's Forbidden Temptation
The Prez's Forbidden Temptation
The Coach's Forbidden Temptation
The Tight End's Forbidden Temptation

The Lucinio Family Series

Available Now

Rising From The Ashes
The Player's Rebel
Encrypting My Heart
Fighting My Fate
Phoenix Rising
Defending Her Honor

Multi Author Series

Piper Falls: Firehouse 49

Available Now

Ignite My Fire by Melony Ann
Regain My Fire by Kindra White
Playing With My Fire by D.L. Howe
Fight My Fire by Darley Collins
Against My Fire by Anneke Boshoff
Relight My Fire by Louise Murchie
Harness My Fire by Ayana Lisbet
Quench My Fire by Havana Wilder

Piper Falls: Station 28 Series

Available Now

Embracing My Duty by Melony Ann
Torn By My Duty by Kayla Baker
Against My Duty by Anneke Boshoff
Defying My Duty by D.L. Howe
Leave Of My Duty by Nikki A. Lamers
Fulfilling My Duty by Havana Wilder
Following My Duty by Louise Murchie
Replete In My Duty by Stacy Kristen
Accepting My Duty by Darley Collins

Snowed In Trilogy

Available Now

Snowed In For Christmas
Snowed In With The Stalker
Snowed In With My Best Friend

Let's Be Friends

Follow me on

Bookbub

Facebook

Goodreads

Instagram

Tik Tok

Visit my website
www.melonyannauthor.com

Subscribe to my newsletter and get a FREE never-seen-before NOVELLA just for subscribers!
https://www.melonyannauthor.com/exclusive-content

Join my Facebook Reader Group!
Melony Ann's Sizzling Book Nook

Acknowledgements

To my loves.

To my friends.

To my team.

To the Bookstagram Community.

To my family.

To all of those who believe in me and support me.

To all of those who don't.

Cover by: Carter Cover Designs

Edited by: Alyssa Skaggs

About Melony Ann

Melony Ann began writing short stories and poetry as a child. She continued honing her craft over the years until she took the plunge and began publishing her work, despite having severe anxiety.

Melony writes contemporary romance stories that are full of suspense and a lot of steam.

When she isn't writing, she is loving her family and working to make her life something she deserves.

Melony believes that if her writing can inspire just one person, then all of her hard work is worth it.

Her hope is that her writing allows each and every one of her readers to escape for a little while. To dive into a different world one book at a time.

www.ingramcontent.com/pod-product-compliance
Lightning Source LLC
LaVergne TN
LVHW010943110826
845149LV00013B/2739
9781961966796